First published in hardback 2010 by Hodder Children's Books
First published in paperback 2011

Text copyright © Catriona Hoy 2010
Illustration copyright © Cassia Thomas 2010

Hodder Children's Books
338 Euston Road
London, NW1 3BH

Hodder Children's Books Australia
Level 17/207 Kent Street
Sydney, NSW 2000

A catalogue record of this book is available
from the British Library.

HB ISBN: 978 0 340 98885 5
PB ISBN: 978 0 340 98886 2
10 9 8 7 6 5 4 3 2 1

Printed in China

Hodder Children's Books
is a division of Hachette
Children's Books,
an Hachette UK Company

www.hachette.co.uk

TO MY WEE SCOTTISH COUSINS...
RYAN, JAMIE, EMILY AND ISLA LU C.H.

FOR M, D, C, L, S AND N, WITH ALL MY LOVE C.T. x

this book belongs to

George and Ghost

and

- - - - - - - - - - - - - -

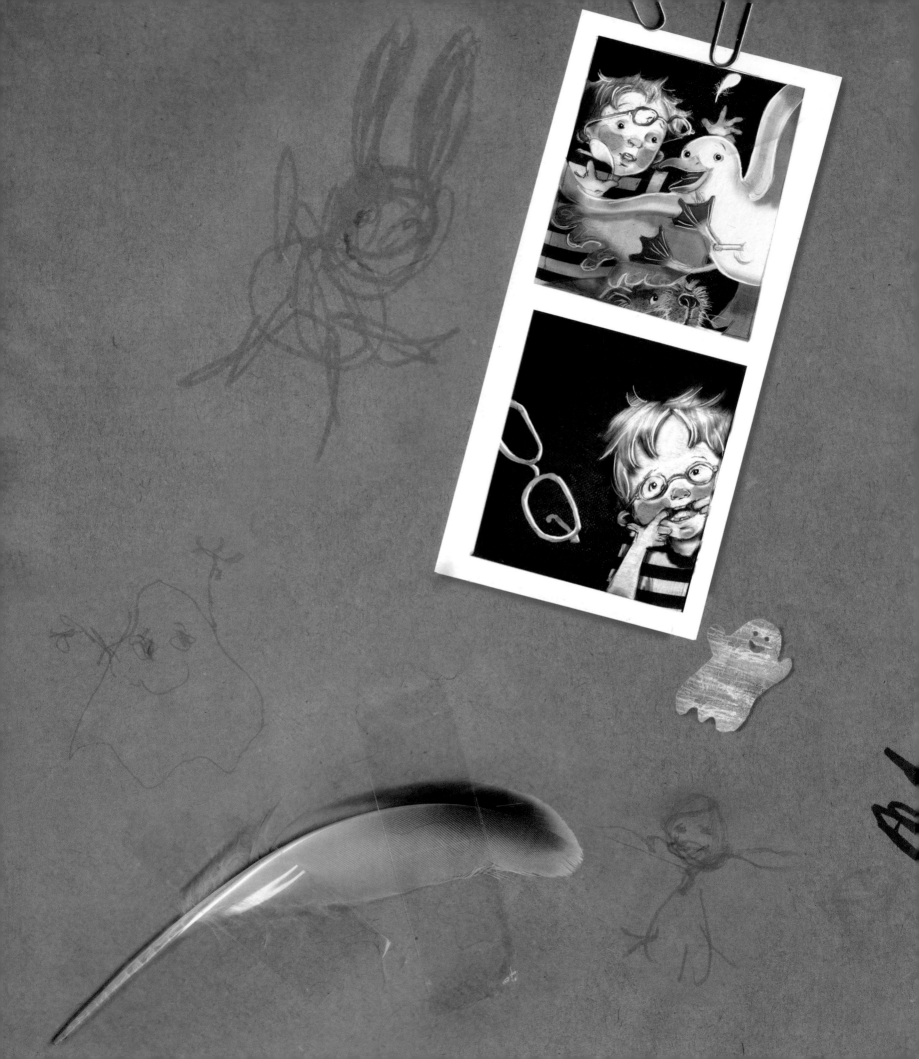

GEORGE
AND GHOST

CATRIONA HOY AND CASSIA THOMAS

Hodder
Children's
Books

A division of Hachette Children's Books

George and Ghost were friends,
but George wasn't sure he
believed in Ghost any more.

'You need to go away,' sighed George. 'You're not real!'

'Prove it,' said Ghost.

George pulled his ear and scratched his head.
'Well, if you were real I could weigh you,'
he said, stepping on to some scales.

'Look, I am real. I weigh something.'
But Ghost didn't weigh anything.

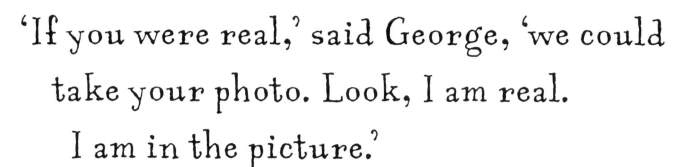

'If you were real,' said George, 'we could take your photo. Look, I am real. I am in the picture.'

But Ghost wasn't in the photo.

'If you were real you would take up space,' said George, filling up a bucket with water.

He stepped into it and the water slopped over. 'Look, I am real. I take up space.'

Ghost stood in the bucket,
but the water didn't spill over.

George and Ghost walked slowly and sadly home.

'You see you really can't be real,' said George.
Ghost sniffed as he waved goodbye.
He felt real.

George thought he saw a tear roll down Ghost's face.

George missed Ghost.

He checked in the cupboard,
but Ghost wasn't there.

He checked up and down, over and under,
in and out, but Ghost still wasn't there.

George cried.

'What's the matter?' asked Ghost,
suddenly appearing.
'I missed you,' said George.
'I missed you too,' said Ghost.

'I've been thinking,' said Ghost,
    'sunshine is real so it should take up space.'

They put sunshine in the bucket,
but it was still empty.

'And thoughts should weigh something,' said Ghost.

They stood on the scales and thought
big thoughts, but the scales didn't move.

'And music is real so we should take
a photo of it,' said Ghost.

They tooted and hooted and took
a photo, but the sounds
were invisible.

'But, most of all, our friendship is real,'
said Ghost as they sat side-by-side.

That night they soon fell fast asleep,
dreaming dreams that weighed nothing
and took up no space at all.

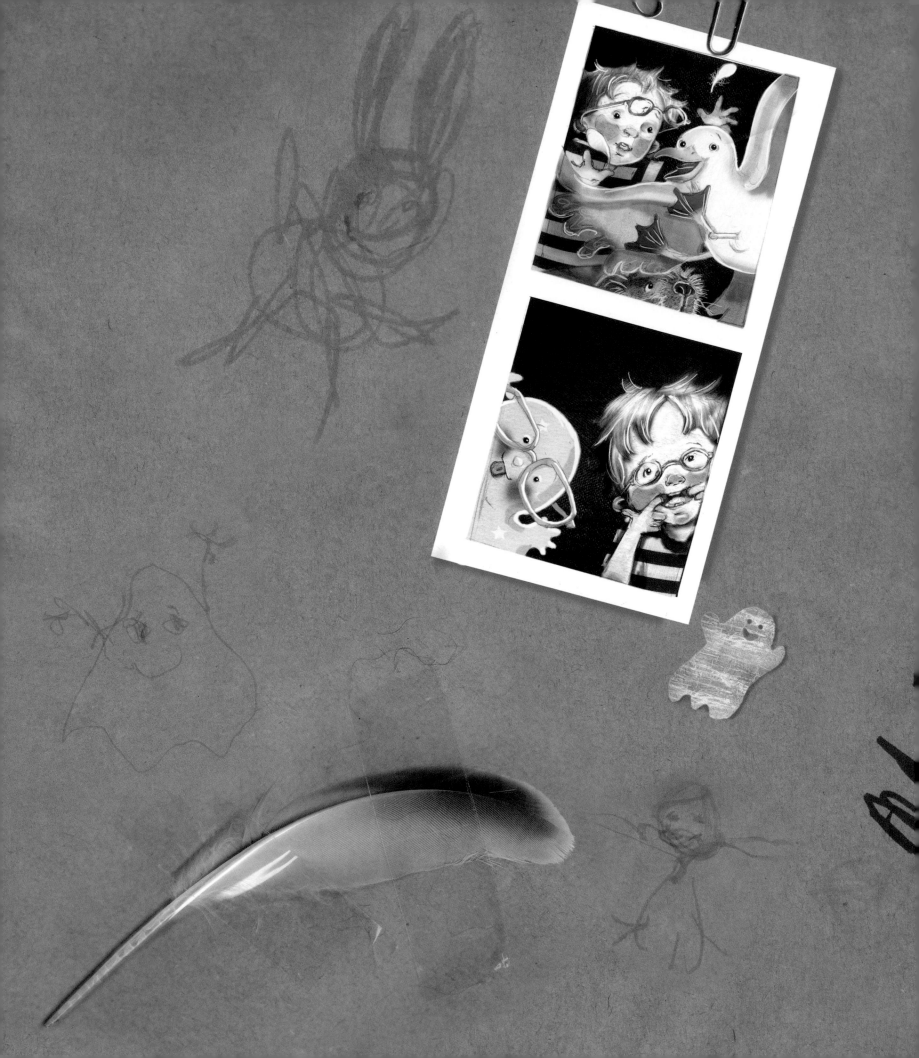

Other great Hodder picture books perfect to share with children:

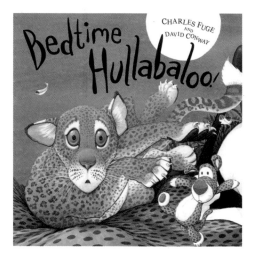

978 0 340 98126 9

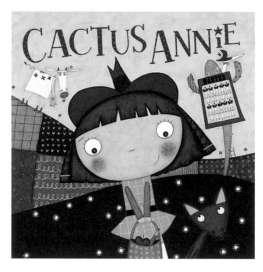

978 0 340 98142 9

978 0 340 98140 5

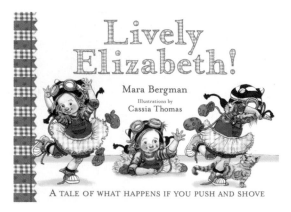

978 0 340 98805 3

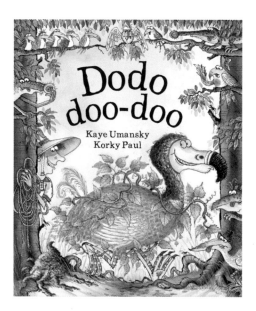

978 0 340 95058 6

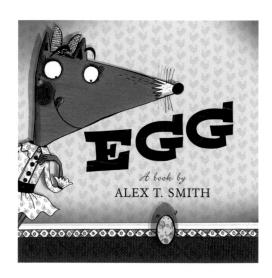

978 0 340 95986 2

Hodder Children's Books

A division of Hachette Children's Books